This book belongs to

....

....

EGMONT

We bring stories to life

First published in Great Britain in 2020 by Egmont UK Limited
2 Minster Court, 10th floor, London EC3R 7BB
www.egmont.co.uk

Written by Katrina Pallant. Designed by Richie Hull and Mark Mitchell.
Illustrated by Robin Davies.

 Thomas the Tank Engine & Friends ™

HiT entertainment   CREATED BY BRITT ALLCROFT

ISBN 978 1 4052 9679 3

70838/001

Printed in China

Egmont takes its responsibility to the planet and its inhabitants
very seriously. We aim to use papers from well-managed forests
run by responsible suppliers.

Stay safe online.
Egmont is not responsible for content hosted by third parties.

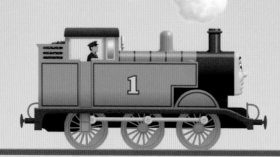

Thomas goes on Safari

This is a story about Thomas, the brave blue engine, and the day he went on an adventure very far from home ...

Thomas was getting ready for a busy day on Sodor when the Fat Controller arrived with some news.

"Thomas, I have a very special job for you this week. You are going to travel to Africa to work with Nia on the Kenyan railway. She has gone on ahead so you will meet her there."

"How exciting!" Thomas thought.

Thomas **puffed** through Sodor on his way to the Docks ...

... where Dilly the Barge was waiting
to transport him across the ocean.

After a long journey, Thomas arrived on the
continent of Africa and headed to Kenya.

Thomas was happy to have arrived at last.

"Hello Thomas!" Nia shouted, as Thomas pulled up. "We are going on a practice run before taking passengers on safari! Hopefully we will see some lions and elephants in their natural habitat."

Thomas knew he should be excited, but he was worried. Weren't elephants **really big?** Didn't lions have **pointed, scary teeth?**

"Don't be scared, Thomas," Nia said.
"We'll start with gentle giraffes."

Thomas and Nia rolled quietly along the track,
through the Kenyan animal reserve, until they
spotted a group of giraffes eating leaves.

Thomas stared up in wonder at the
tallest creatures he'd ever seen.

"Giraffes can grow to **6 metres tall**," Nia explained. "That's taller than a double-decker bus!"

Thomas and Nia rolled on visiting the animals on the reserve.

Thomas couldn't believe it when Nia told him zebras could run up to **65 kilometres** per hour. Faster than Bertie the bus!

"Did you know elephants can drink over **200 litres** of water per day?" Nia said. Almost as much as fills a swimming pool!

Nia warned Thomas that visitors should not get too close to the rhinos.

Thomas was amazed by all the different animals, but he was still worried about the **roaring** lions and **big** elephants.

Just then, a giant hippo appeared out of the river with a ...

Splash!

Thomas was scared. He imagined the hippo was coming after him. He **peeped** his whistle and sped away up the track.

Nia **chugged** after Thomas. She tried to tell him that the hippo wasn't chasing him.

But it was too late. Thomas rolled so fast up the track that he didn't see the trouble ahead.

There had been a landslide and now Thomas was **stuck in the mud!**

"Why did you go so fast, Thomas?" Nia asked when she arrived. "Not to worry, I'll go and get the towrope to pull you out."

"Sorry, Nia. I was scared and went too fast."
Thomas was embarrassed.

But instead of digging Thomas out, Nia's crew started putting
more mud on him. "On hot days, hippos coat themselves in mud,"
Nia explained. "This will keep you cool while I fetch help."

When Nia returned to tow Thomas out of the mud, he was **dirtier than he had ever been!**

"I stayed nice and cool thanks to your idea with the mud," Thomas said. "Those hippos are clever."

Nia pulled him free and took him to be
washed down by a friendly elephant.
Thomas was no longer scared of this
giant but gentle creature.

Nia took Thomas back to the river to show him a family of hippos. He realised they weren't scary either, as long as you didn't get too close!

"There is a lot **we can learn** from the animals if we pay attention," replied Nia.

After their practice run, Nia and Thomas took lots of passengers on safari. Everyone had a great time and Thomas even conquered his fear of lions!

The engines were ready to head home. "I've learned more about the animals and I hope to come again soon," Thomas said. He peeped goodbye to Kenya.

Thomas and Nia arrived back on Sodor, excited to see all their friends.

As Thomas puffed back to the Tidmouth Sheds, ready to have a long sleep, he saw the sheep and cows in the fields.

"I can have a safari right here in Sodor," Thomas laughed.

"It's fun visiting new places, but **it's good to be home.**"

About the author

The Reverend W. Awdry was the creator of 26 little books about Thomas and his famous engine friends, the first being published in 1945. The stories came about when the Reverend's two-year-old son Christopher was ill in bed with the measles. Awdry invented stories to amuse him, which Christopher then asked to hear time and time again. And now for over 75 years, children all around the world have been asking to hear these stories about Thomas, Edward, Gordon, James and the many other Really Useful Engines.

THE RAILWAY SERIES
THE THREE RAILWAY ENGINES

The Reverend W. Awdry with so[...]
readers at a model railway exhib[...]